Benjy's Dog House

Margaret Bloy Graham

SCHOLASTIC BOOK SERVICES
NEW YORK · TORONTO · LONDON · AUCKLAND · SYDNEY · TOKYO

ISBN: 0-590-10118-8

Copyright © 1973 by Margaret Bloy Graham. This edition is published by Scholastic Book Services, a division of Scholastic Magazines, Inc., by arrangement with Harper & Row, Publishers, Inc.

14 13 12 11 10 9 8 7 6   01/8

Printed in the U.S.A.

07

Benjy's Dog House

Benjy was a brown dog with long ears and a short tail.

He lived with Father, Mother, Linda, and Jimmy.

Every evening when Linda and Jimmy went to bed,

Benjy went to bed too.

Sometimes he slept on Linda's bed,

and sometimes he slept on Jimmy's.
Benjy loved going to bed.

One day Father said, "Benjy's not a puppy anymore.

I think it's about time he slept outside.

Let's make that old apple barrel into a dog house."

Father brought the barrel out of the cellar.

Jimmy put bricks on either side to keep it from rolling,

and Linda painted it. Then Mother put a blanket inside,

and the dog house was finished.

Everybody stood around admiring it—
everybody, that is, except Benjy.

That night at bedtime, Father put Benjy in the dog house.

"Now go to sleep," he said.

But Benjy couldn't sleep. It was dark out there,

and he missed Linda and Jimmy.

He got up, went to the back door, and whined and whined.

But nobody came to let him in.

Benjy decided to look for somewhere else to sleep.

He went to the main street of town

and stopped at the all-night diner.

"No dogs allowed in here," said the owner.

Benjy went to the firehouse.

"Can't come in here," said the fireman.

"Spot hates other dogs."

He went to the police station.

"Better go home, doggie," said the policeman.

Benjy turned and walked slowly down the street.

All at once Benjy saw a light in the bakery.

He ran over and barked at the door.

"Come on in," said the baker. "Nice to have a visitor.

My cat ran away weeks ago—it's been lonely

around here without her."

The baker gave Benjy
a meat pie

and fixed him a bed
of empty flour sacks.

Benjy spent the night in the warm, cozy bakery.

Early next morning he went home, rested and cheerful.

From then on, Benjy spent his days with the family

and his nights with the baker.

Benjy was happy. So were Father and Mother—

they thought he slept in his dog house every night.

But Linda and Jimmy weren't happy. They missed Benjy.

One night Benjy went to the bakery as usual.

The moment he walked through the door

a howling ball of fur flew at him.

Benjy was so surprised he couldn't even move—

and he got a scratch on the nose.

The baker came running.

"Cut it out, Kitty!" he yelled,

and chased the cat away.

"My cat came back today with kittens," said the baker.

"Sorry, but you can't come here anymore, pal.

Here's a present for you."

He gave Benjy a paper bag.

Benjy took the bag

and walked slowly out the door and down the street.

Now he'd have to sleep in that dark, lonely dog house.

When Benjy got back, he put down the bag
and just sat there. He felt miserable.

All at once he sniffed the bag. Meat pies!
He ate one. It tasted so good . . .

that he ate another one, and another, and another

till all the meat pies were gone!

Then he curled up to go to sleep.

But in a little while . . .

Benjy began to have an awful stomach ache.

He tossed and turned

and had bad dreams all night long.

In the morning he didn't even get up.

"Poor Benjy's sick," said Jimmy.

"Look, there's a bag from the bakery," said Linda.

"Maybe he took something and ate it," said Mother.

"I think you'd better go and see the baker after school."

That afternoon the children went to the bakery.

Benjy went too. He was feeling better.

"Our dog took this bag from your store," said Linda.

"We want to pay for it," said Jimmy.

"Say, that's my friend!" cried the baker.

"I *gave* him that bag—full of meat pies.

He used to stay with me every night, but that's all over."

The baker took them to the back room.

"My cat came back yesterday with kittens," he said.

"You'd better keep your dog home, or he'll get scratched."

"Don't worry," said Linda and Jimmy. "We will!"

When they got home, Linda said, "The baker gave Benjy

a bag of meat pies. Benjy used to go there every night."

"I bet he was lonely," said Jimmy. "Please let him sleep

in the house again, Dad."

"Maybe you're right," said Father. "Maybe Benjy was lonely.

It's all right with me if he sleeps inside again."

"Hurray!" cried the children, and Benjy wagged his tail.

That night Benjy slept on Jimmy's bed,

and the next night he slept on Linda's.

It was just like old times.

A few days later, Jimmy and Linda

made Benjy's dog house into a strawberry barrel.

They made holes in the barrel, filled it with earth,

and planted strawberry plants in the holes.

Benjy watched happily. Now he knew for sure

he'd never ever have to sleep in that old barrel again!